Lee Aucoin, *Creative Director*
Jamey Acosta, *Senior Editor*
Heidi Fiedler, *Editor*
Produced and designed by
Denise Ryan & Associates
Illustration © Susy Boyer
Rachelle Cracchiolo, *Publisher*

Teacher Created Materials
5301 Oceanus Drive
Huntington Beach, CA 92649-1030
http://www.tcmpub.com
Paperback: ISBN: 978-1-4333-5530-1
Library Binding: ISBN: 978-1-4807-1698-8
© 2014 Teacher Created Materials

Boris
and Bea

Written by Sharon Callen
Illustrated by Susy Boyer

Boris the Basset and Bea were best friends. Bea
got Boris from her Aunt Kay, an animal doctor.

Boris and Bea exercised together. They read books together. They listened to music together. They even ate dinner together.

4

Every day, Bea brushed Boris. He wagged
his tail with joy. He loved being brushed.

Every night, Bea tucked Boris into his basket next to her bed. He snored happily. He loved to sleep near Bea.

But whenever Bea took Boris for a walk outside, he never wagged his tail. Bea was worried. What could be wrong?

"Boris is a healthy dog. And he loves you," Aunt Kay told Bea.

"Then, why doesn't he like going for walks? Why doesn't he play with the other dogs?" asked Bea. "When I take him to Pooch Park, he just sits and watches. He never plays with the other dogs. Sometimes, he just doesn't seem happy."

Bea took Boris to visit Aunt Kay at the clinic. Aunt Kay checked his ears, his eyes, and his paws. She even checked his heart. He was perfectly healthy.

"When Boris was my dog, he used to be a therapy dog," said Aunt Kay.

"What kind of dog is that? I thought he was a basset hound," said Bea.

12

"Therapy dogs visit children in the hospital. They sit with each child and help them feel better."

"So he grew up inside, walking around the hospital!" said Bea.

14

"Yes. He grew up with lots of people!
I think he loves people more than he loves dogs,"
said Aunt Kay.

"Why did you give Boris to me?" asked Bea.

"Boris especially loves children. So when you were old enough to look after a pet, I knew he would be the perfect present for you. I knew you would be the best of friends," said Aunt Kay.

Bea hugged Aunt Kay. "Can Boris be a therapy dog again?" Bea asked. "I think he misses all the children."

"I'm sure he would like that," said Aunt Kay.

19

So every day on her way to school, Bea walked Boris to the children's hospital.

He sat with each child for a while. He
made them feel much happier.

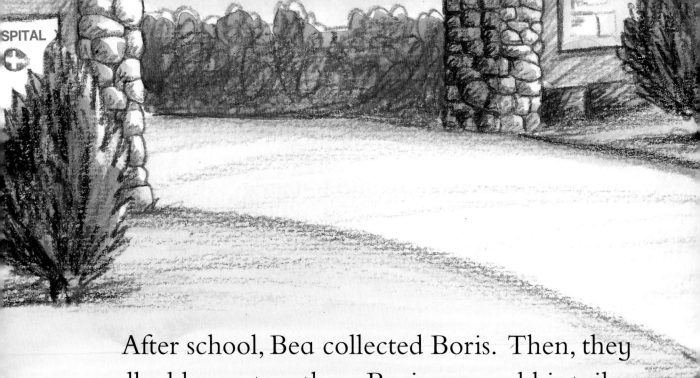

After school, Bea collected Boris. Then, they walked home together. Boris wagged his tail every time. He no longer looked sad.

And when they got home, they did things together. Just like they always did.

Boris was very happy. And so was Bea.